*For George and Alex and all
our escaped hamsters – JH*

*For Mum and Dad, thanks for
your support, love Jamie*

First Published in Great Britain in 1997
Bloomsbury Publishing Plc, 38 Soho Square, London W1V 5DF

Copyright © Text Jillian Harker 1997
Copyright © Illustrations Jamie Smith 1997
Art Direction Lisa Coombes

ISBN 0 7475 3053 X

Printed by Bath Press, Great Britain

10 9 8 7 6 5 4 3 2 1

Little Readers

Can't
Catch
Me!

Jillian Harker

Pictures by Jamie Smith

Bloomsbury Children's Books

"Please, Mrs Baxter," said Robby. "Nibbles is gone."
Everyone stopped what they were doing.
The classroom went silent.
"Gone?" said Mrs Baxter.
And she looked straight at Tom.

TODAY
TOM
WILL FEED NIBBLES

"Tom," she said, **"did you feed Nibbles this morning?"**

"Yes, miss," mumbled Tom. "I did it during register."

He looked down at the floor. His face went very red.

"I m-m-must have left the d-d-door open."

All the children jumped from their seats. Jane and Suzy searched the shelf. They hunted behind the books.

I've been looking for that rubber!

Martin and Sam crawled under the tables. Lawrence emptied out his bag. A big tear trickled down Sarah's nose.

Mrs Baxter sighed loudly.

"He's been over here," shouted Daisy, holding up
a piece of paper. "Mark and I can follow the clues."
Mark nodded.

He went over to the science cupboard and took out two magnifying glasses. Daisy and Mark began to look for clues.
"Perhaps you could mop up the paint first," said Mrs Baxter.

"He's been over here,"
called Suzy, holding up a pencil.
"Look at these teethmarks."

Everyone came rushing over.

"There he is," Suzy
whispered. "He's behind
the bookcase."

Sam and Sarah had an idea. They fetched an old
curtain from the dressing-up box.
"We'll just sit here quietly," said Sarah,
" and wait for him to come out."

He's too
fast for
that!

"Well, that idea didn't
work," said Sam.

"Don't worry, Mrs Baxter," said Jane.
"Some of us are going to build a conTRAPtion."
"We'll catch him," said Robby.

The children from Blue Group tipped all the construction toys on to the floor. It wasn't long before they'd built a huge trap.

But Nibbles gave them the slip. "Well, that idea didn't work," said Robby. "Now he's gone into that hole."

"He loves his hamster ball," said Martin.

He's too clever for that!

"We could leave it in front of the hole and slip the lid on when he goes in."

He put the ball carefully in front of the hole.

But Nibbles fooled them.
"Oh no!" they all said.
"Look at that!"
"Well, that idea didn't
work," said Tom.

"What are you
doing, Tom?" asked Mrs Baxter crossly.
"You haven't helped at all.
And you were the one who left the cage door open."

"Please, Mrs Baxter," said Tom quietly.
"I have an idea."
Tom put his finger to his lips. The classroom
went silent. He walked over to the carpet, sat
down, and held out his hand.

"Can you get him back into the cage, Tom?" whispered Mrs Baxter. Tom nodded.

This tastes good!

Everyone cheered. **"Well done, Tom!"** said Mrs Baxter.
She called all the children on to the carpet.
"Now we really must get on," she said. **"We've
wasted nearly a whole morning."**

Suzy's hand went up. "Please, miss, can I draw a picture
of Tom and Nibbles?" she asked.
"We'd like to make a better trap," said Jane and Robby.
"Could we write a story about Nibbles?" asked Mark.
"I've got an idea for a poem," said Daisy.

In no time at all,
everyone was busy working.
Nibbles was safely back in his cage.

"Tell me something, Tom," asked Mrs Baxter.
"How did you know what to do?"

"Easy," said Tom. "I just read all about it."

"Well!" said Mrs Baxter at the end of the day.
**"Perhaps it wasn't such a bad thing that Tom
left the cage door open, after all."**